Seven at One Blow

A Tale from the Brothers Grimm

retold by **ERIC A. KIMMEL**

illustrated by **MEGAN LLOYD**

HOLIDAY HOUSE ❧ **NEW YORK**

To Madeline — E. A. K.

To the Dietrichs, thanks to our fine Fiona,
who can also swat seven at one blow. Moo! — M. L.

AUTHOR'S NOTE

Seven at One Blow, or *The Gallant Little Tailor (Das tapfere Schneiderlein)* appeared in the
first volume of Grimm's Fairy Tales, published in 1812. The tailor is one of the most
appealing characters in Grimm. There is nothing heroic about him, but because he pos-
sesses such supreme self-confidence he inevitably becomes the hero he pretends to be.
As the saying goes: whether you say you can or can't, you're right.

Text copyright © 1998 by Eric A. Kimmel
Illustrations copyright © 1998 by Megan Lloyd-Thompson
All Rights Reserved
Printed in the United States of America. Book design by Sylvia Frezzolini Severance.
FIRST EDITION
Library of Congress Cataloguing-in-Publication Data
Kimmel, Eric A.
Seven at one blow: a tale from the Brothers Grimm / retold by Eric A. Kimmel; illustrated by Megan Lloyd.
p. cm.
Summary: Relates how a tailor who kills seven flies at one blow manages to become king.
ISBN 0-8234-1383-7
[1. Fairy tales. 2. Folklore—Germany.] I. Grimm, Jacob, 1785–1863. II. Grimm, Wilhelm, 1786–1859.
III. Lloyd, Megan, ill. IV. Brave little tailor. English. V. Title.
PZ8.K527Se 1998
398.2'0943'02—dc21   97–44200
[E]   CIP
                                                   AC

One afternoon a tailor sat sewing by his
window. He heard a woman in the street
crying, "Fine jelly to sell!"

"I'll buy some," the tailor called down.

The woman lugged her jelly basket up the stairs.
The tailor opened the jars so he could taste each one.

"I'll take one teaspoon of blackberry jelly,"
the tailor finally said.

The woman measured out
the jelly and left, furious at having
to lug her jars up the six flights
of stairs to sell one teaspoon.
But the tailor didn't care.
He spread the jelly over a thick
slice of bread and returned to
his sewing.

Nothing draws flies like jelly. Soon, all the flies in the neighborhood had gathered for a taste.

"Who invited you?" the tailor cried.
He swatted the flies with a towel,
leaving seven lying dead in the jelly.
    "Seven at one blow! What a feat!
The world must know of this."

The tailor embroidered his belt with bright gold letters:

Seven at One Blow

"One who has killed seven at one blow is far too grand to be a tailor," he decided. So he laid down his needle and set out into the world to seek his fortune.

He carried a cheese in his pocket. Along the way he found a wren caught in a thorn bush. The tailor put her in his pocket, too, and continued on his way.

Soon he came to a mountain, which turned out to be no mountain at all, but an enormous giant.

"Good day to you!" the tailor sang out.

The giant raised his club. "Miserable creeper! I'll smash you!"

"Read this first." The tailor opened his coat to reveal:

SEVEN AT ONE BLOW

Seven at one blow? That could mean men . . . or giants. The giant never suspected it meant flies.

"Are you strong? Can you do this?" The giant squeezed a stone until water ran out.

"Nothing is easier." The tailor took his cheese and squeezed it until the whey ran down his arm.

"That was too easy," the giant said. He picked up another stone and hurled it high in the air. "Can you do that?" he asked the tailor.

"Your stone fell back to earth," the tailor replied. "I will throw mine so high it will never return." He took the wren out of his pocket and threw her into the air. The little bird took wing and flew away.

The frightened giant decided to make friends with the tailor, planning to kill him later. "You may spend the night in my cave, if you help me carry some firewood," the giant said.

The giant pulled a huge tree out of the ground. "Which end do you want to carry?" he asked the tailor.

"I'll take the leaves and the branches. That's the most difficult part."

The giant hoisted the tree onto his shoulders. The moment he turned around, the tailor swung himself into the branches, so that the giant carried the whole tree and the tailor besides.

The merry tailor began to sing, "*A jolly tailor went a'roving . . .*"

The giant turned around. The tailor leaped down and pretended to hold up the branches.

"Is this load so light you can sing?" the giant asked.

"It's not heavy at all," the tailor replied.

On they went, the tailor whistling and singing as if the tree weighed no more than a handkerchief. The giant sweated and grunted with every step. He never suspected he was carrying the entire load.

They reached the giant's cave after dark.
The giant's brothers came out to greet them.

"Who is this insect? We'll grind his bones!"
they growled at the tailor.

"Take care, brothers," the giant whispered. "This little
fellow has killed seven at one blow."

The tailor showed the giants his belt. Like their brother,
they assumed that seven at one blow meant men or giants.
They never suspected the seven were only flies.

"It's time to sleep," the giants said.

"Take my bed," the first giant told the
tailor. The giants lay down and were soon
snoring loud enough to shake the mountains.

But the tailor couldn't sleep a wink.
"This bed is hard as stones," he said to himself.
He crawled into one of the giant's socks, which
made a fine sleeping bag.

The giants awoke at midnight. Taking iron bars,
they smashed the bed where they thought the tailor lay.
They battered it until nothing remained but splinters
and mattress stuffing.

"That's the end of him. Seven at one blow indeed!"

At dawn they discovered the tailor sitting in the wrecked bed, scratching himself all over.

"This bed is full of fleas!" he exclaimed. "They bit me from head to foot. I hardly slept a wink."

The giants fled, leaving behind all their treasures, for they thought their savage blows meant no more to the tailor than a few flea bites. The tailor helped himself to a fine sword, a purse of gold coins, and a knapsack of bread and mutton.

Then he set off boldly on his way,
for one who has killed seven at one blow
need not be afraid of anyone.

Soon the tailor arrived at a kingdom ravaged by two ogres. The tailor came before the king and said, "What will you give me if I slay these ogres for you?"

The king laughed. "These ogres have overcome my bravest knights. How can you hope to defeat them?"

The tailor opened his coat. The king read:

SEVEN AT ONE BLOW

The king promised his daughter in marriage and the kingdom after his death if the tailor could kill the ogres.

The tailor set out for the forest. He found the ogres sleeping beneath an oak tree. The tailor climbed the tree.

Seating himself on a branch, he dropped an acorn on
the first ogre's head. The ogre opened his eyes. "Keep your
hands to yourself," he growled at his companion.

"I didn't touch you!" the second ogre protested.

"Don't let it happen again," the first ogre warned him.

The ogres went back to sleep. The tailor
dropped another acorn on the second ogre's forehead.
The ogre struck his companion on the nose.

"How dare you hit me!"

"You hit me first!"

"You started it!"

"No, you did!"

The enraged ogres uprooted trees. They battered
each other until both lay dead.

When the king's men arrived, they found the tailor sitting on a tree trunk with two dead ogres at his feet.

The king was not pleased to see the tailor return. One who had killed two ogres and had slain seven at one blow could be dangerous. What if he decided to seize the crown before the king was dead? Best to get rid of him, quietly and quickly.

The king told the tailor, "I have another task for you. A ferocious unicorn is ravishing my kingdom. Can you capture him for me?"

"One who has slain seven at one blow is hardly afraid of a unicorn," the tailor replied. Taking a rope and an ax, he set out for the forest. The king watched him go, hoping he would never come back.

The tailor strolled through the forest. Suddenly, he heard a roar. Looking around, he saw the unicorn coming straight at him. The tailor threw himself on the ground.

The unicorn charged over him and ran his horn through a tree.

"Don't be afraid, unicorn. I won't hurt you." The tailor spoke
softly until the unicorn lost his fear. Then he tied the rope around the
unicorn's neck, cut down the tree, and led the unicorn back to the king like
a dog on a leash.

This made the king more determined than ever to get rid of the
tailor. He said to him, "A wild boar is devastating my kingdom.
Capture him and I will be forever in your debt."

"You already are,"
the tailor warned. "We will
celebrate the wedding when
I return. If not, you will have
to reckon with one who has
killed seven at one blow."

The tailor returned to the
forest. While passing near an
abandoned chapel, he heard a
great snorting and grunting.
It was the wild boar.

The boar charged at the tailor.
The tailor ran as fast as he could, with
the boar's tusks slashing at his heels.
Six times they ran around the chapel.
On the seventh time the tailor ran
through the door and hopped out the
window. The boar chased him inside,
but he was too huge to fit through the
window himself. The tailor ran around
to the door and slammed it shut.
The king's men arrived to find the
boar trapped inside the chapel.
"He's quite harmless now. Do
what you like with him,"
the tailor said.

The king dared not delay the wedding this time.
The tailor married the king's daughter and settled
down to live happily ever after.

Then one night the princess heard her new husband talking in his sleep.

"Ho, boy! Stitch me that waistcoat and hem me those trousers, or I'll lay my yardstick around your shoulders!"

The princess recoiled with indignation. "He isn't a prince; he isn't even a nobleman. He's just a common tailor!"

The next morning she demanded to be released from her marriage.

"Softly, softly," the king said. "We must handle this fellow with care. Tailor or not, he has killed seven at one blow. Leave your door unlocked tonight. I will send my henchmen to murder him in his sleep. You may marry whomever you like once he is dead."

The king's page overheard these words. The boy admired the gallant tailor, who had always treated him kindly. The page warned the tailor of the plot against him.

"Don't worry about me," the tailor said. "One who has slain seven at one blow is not afraid of anyone."

That night the tailor pretended to sleep. The moment he heard the bedroom door creak open, he shouted in a loud voice, "Ho, boy! Stitch me that waistcoat and hem me those trousers, or I'll lay my yardstick around your shoulders! I have slain seven at one blow, driven out three giants, killed two ogres, captured a unicorn and a savage boar. Why should I fear those cowards lurking in the hallway?"

The king's henchmen took to their heels. The princess fled with them. So did the king. They ran away in the middle of the night and never returned.

The king's former subjects chose the tailor to be their new king, reasoning that anyone who has slain seven at one blow ought to make a good one.

And indeed he did.